Nov.,
2000

Dear Roxann,

Someday you will
grow into these books
and will read them all by
yourself.

Love,
Aunt Lois & Uncle Frank

Frank Fister's Hidden Talent

story and pictures by
Paul Brett Johnson

Orchard Books   New York

Orchard Books, 95 Madison Avenue, New York, NY 10016

Manufactured in the United States of America. Printed by Barton Press, Inc.
Bound by Horowitz/Rae. Book design by Mina Greenstein
The text of this book is set in 14 point ITC Bookman. The illustrations are acrylic
paintings reproduced in full color.   10 9 8 7 6 5 4 3 2 1

Library of Congress Cataloging-in-Publication Data
Johnson, Paul Brett. Frank Fister's hidden talent : story and pictures / by Paul Brett
Johnson.   p.   cm. "A Richard Jackson book"—Half t.p.
Summary: Frank's ability to stop things from working when he makes a funny face
causes him to be kidnapped by a greedy chicken thief.
ISBN 0-531-06813-7.   ISBN 0-531-08663-1 (lib. bdg.)
[1. Robbers and outlaws—Fiction.   2. Kidnapping—Fiction.   3. Magic—Fiction.]
I. Title. PZ7.J6354Fr 1994 [E]—dc20 93-4883

For Brett
and for John, Lisa, and Syd

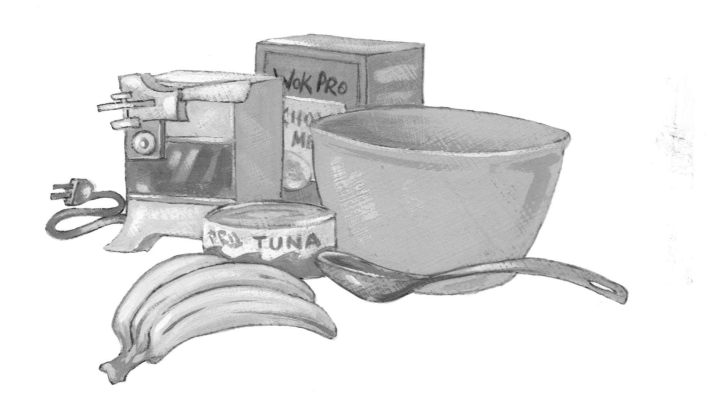

Whenever Frank Fister crossed his eyes and stuck out his tongue at the same time, he could make things not work.

Frank discovered this ability quite by accident. His mom was making banana-tuna chow mein—again. Frank did what anyone might have done under the circumstances. He crossed his eyes and stuck out his tongue. At that very moment the can opener quit.

"Did I do that?" he asked himself, amazed.

Frank tried his hidden talent on the way to school
next morning. Mean Homer Snedge was shooting
spitballs in the back of the bus. As soon as Frank crossed
his eyes and stuck out his tongue, Homer's rubber band
backfired. It sent a spitball flying up Homer's nose.

To be absolutely, positively sure of his talent, Frank tried it again after school. His sister was watching one of those love stories. Frank made the necessary face, and the TV blinked off.

Wow! This is awesome! Frank thought. The best part was that no one had caught on to what Frank was doing. His mom blamed the can opener. Homer Snedge blamed the rubber band. And his sister blamed the TV.

Saturday came warm and sunny. Frank and his dog, Rusty, were out in the yard playing tackle when a familiar sound caught their attention. *Ding-ding-ding.* The Mister Freezee truck rounded the corner and slowly clanged up the street. It stopped in the middle of the block.

Almost on its own, a sneaky plan began to form in Frank's mind.

As the neighborhood kids crowded around, Frank shook his head. "Nah, I really shouldn't," he told himself. But he just couldn't resist the urge.

The ice cream spigots would not shut off! To avoid a sticky mess, Mister Freezee had to fill cones and give them away as fast as he could. The crowd cheered.

You would expect an ice cream man to be the nicest sort of person. You might even expect an ice cream man to forgive a lowdown trick like Frank's. But Mister Freezee was not really an ice cream man. And he was anything but nice. In truth, Mister Freezee was an out-of-work chicken thief who was selling ice cream only to make ends meet. Mister Freezee wasn't even his real name.

Having a criminal mind, the so-called Mister Freezee caught on to Frank in a flash. He realized Frank had a hidden talent. That boy could be a gold mine, he thought.

So after the ice cream had run out and the crowd
had broken up, Mister Freezee kidnapped Frank and
Rusty. He tied Frank's hands behind his back and
slapped a piece of tape across his mouth—"so you don't
try anything funny with that tricky tongue," he growled.
Then he climbed in the driver's seat and sped away.

Mister Freezee took Frank and Rusty to his shabby apartment. He shoved them through the door.

"I've been waiting a long time for a break like this," Mr. Freezee snarled. "So you better cooperate, kid. You wouldn't want anything to happen to your dog."

Frank scowled back at Mr. Freezee.

"You better do as I say. Understand, kid?"

For Rusty's sake, Frank nodded yes.

Mister Freezee continued. "Me and you're gonna pay a visit to Happy Cluck Chicken Farm. When I give the word, you're gonna use that hidden talent of yours to kill the alarm. Got it?"

Frank closed his eyes and tried to figure a way out of this mess.

"Remember . . . do anything foolish and it's all over for the mutt." Mister Freezee collected a few chicken-thieving things before they returned to the ice cream truck and headed for the country.

The robbery went without a hitch. After Mister
Freezee made the guard lie face-down, he yanked the tape
from Frank's mouth. "Do your stuff, kid!" he yelled.

The following morning Mister Freezee laughed with glee at the headlines:

ICE CREAM MAN AND YOUNG BOY HIT CHICKEN FARM.
ALARM MALFUNCTIONS.

"We got a terrific future, kid."
With his mouth retaped, Frank could only moan.
How could he ever face his friends again? Frank worried
about his parents, too. By now they must be frantic.

That afternoon Mister Freezee had to go out for chicken feed. The chickens were restless and feathers were flying.

Mister Freezee narrowed his eyes and looked hard at Frank. "No monkey business while I'm out." He tied Frank to a chair, then left and locked the door behind him.

When Frank could no longer hear footsteps, he tried
every way possible to free himself. But the knots held
firm. Still Frank continued to twist and squirm.

Then Frank's chair toppled backwards. Rusty came
bounding over. Was this a new game? He wanted to join,
but he was confused. Not knowing what else to do, Rusty
gave Frank a wet sloppy kiss with his big rough tongue
right across the mouth. Then he gave him another one.
And another.

"Way to go, big guy!" Frank cried gratefully when the
tape was loosened from his mouth. Rusty seemed pleased
with himself.

Frank looked directly at the ropes that bound his arms and chest. He crossed his eyes and stuck out his tongue. As if by magic, the knots came undone and the ropes fell away.

When Mister Freezee returned with both arms full, he got a real surprise.

"Rusty! Tackle!" Frank commanded. Mister Freezee went sprawling.

Rusty sat on top of the evil chicken thief and growled his worst growl while Frank called 911.

The next day the headlines read,

FRANK FISTER FOILS FOWL FELON.

Frank and Rusty were heroes.

Frank's mom beamed. "Your father and I are so proud of you, dear. You have made the world a better place."

To celebrate, Frank's mom prepared a surprise for dinner. Liver-and-onion cheesecake. Frank groaned silently. But he was careful not to make any faces.

Later, however, Frank did cross his eyes and stick out his tongue. He did it in front of the bedroom mirror to put an end to his hidden talent.

"Enough abracadabra," he said. "Let's stick with the *real* world."

Rusty thumped his tail in agreement.